ADVENTURES IN THE KINGDOM™

ARMOR OF LIGHT

Written by Dian Layton
Illustrations created by Al Berg

The people who walked in Darkness
Have seen a great Light!
Those who walked in the dragon's land
Upon them the Light has shined!
That's verse 2 of Isaiah 9!
That's verse 2 of Isaiah 9.

Moira

The King

Seeker

Gladness

Glee

Giggles

Do

Doodle

Yes

Dawdle

Slow

HopeSo

KnowSo

Illustrations created by Al Berg.

Published by MercyPlace Ministries

MercyPlace is a licensed imprint of Destiny Image® Inc.

Distributed by

Destiny Image® Publishers, Inc.
P.O. Box 310
Shippensburg, PA 17257-0310

ISBN 0-9707919-7-6

For Worldwide Distribution
Printed in the U.S.A.

This book and all other Destiny Image, Revival Press, MercyPlace, Fresh Bread, Destiny Image Fiction, and Treasure House books are available at Christian bookstores and distributors worldwide.

For a U.S. bookstore nearest you, call **1-800-722-6774**.
For more information on foreign distributors, call **717-532-3040**.
Or reach us on the Internet: **www.seeker.org**

CONTENTS

CHAPTER ONE

Seeker knocked again. "Please, Moira, can I come in? Just for a few minutes?"

There was no response; so he knocked another time. "Moira, I REALLY want to talk to you! Please?!"

Seeker heard Moira sigh a deep sigh, "Oh...all right."

Seeker walked in, and there was his sister. Her eyes were red and puffy, and soggy tissues were scattered all over the bed. Seeker found a place among the soggy tissues and sat down. "Moira, what's wrong? What's the matter? Ever since you came back to the Kingdom you've been so sad! And I thought you would be so happy! I was looking forward to all the adventures we would go on together."

Moira turned her puffy eyes toward him and said with a sob, "Oh, Seeker, I can't forget them!"

"Forget who?"

"I can't forget all the people I met when I lived in the World Beyond the Kingdom! Oh, Seeker, it's awful out there. It's so dark, and so empty; and I'm sure that I saw some dragons hiding throughout the streets and alleys. Ugh! It was as if those horrible creatures were just waiting for their chance to grab people! The people...the people don't know about the King, Seeker. They don't even know that there's a Kingdom!

"I keep thinking and thinking about them; I remember their faces, and I just hurt inside. Especially this one friend I had—her name was Loneliness. She told me once that she had a son— but whenever I asked about him, she would whisper, 'So many regrets. So many regrets...' Isn't that sad, Seeker? And I don't even know what his name was."

Moira paused for a moment to blow her nose, then continued. "Loneliness was with me in the Valley of Lost Dreams when the King found me...and I just left her there! How could I do that? Why didn't I ask her to come to the Kingdom with me?"

Moira sighed another deep sigh. "Anyway, I remember Loneliness, and I remember all the other people and Seeker, I just hurt inside."

"Moira, what you need is a Secret Place!"

"A Secret Place?" she echoed.

2

"Yeah, a Secret Place," said Seeker. "Don't you remember how you and I used to go there together? Don't you remember how we fought the dragons that were holding Dad in chains?!"

Moira nodded slowly. "That all seems so long ago, Seeker, but I do remember."

"Well, I have a Secret Place in one of the towers of the Castle; and I'm the only one who has the key to that room. I can go there any time I want and the King is always there. I don't always see him, but he is always there." Seeker moved closer to his sister and put an arm around her shoulders. "If you go to your Secret Place, Moira, you can tell the King how much you hurt inside, and he'll tell you what to do."

"Oh Seeker," Moira said as she blew her nose again, "that's a great idea. I've just stayed in here crying, but I haven't cried out to the King! I'm going to find my own special Secret Place right now!"

Moira stood to her feet and walked toward the door; then she paused and turned back. "Thanks, little brother." she said, and gave Seeker a warm hug.

"You're welcome, Moira."

After Moira had gone, Seeker continued to sit quietly in her room, thinking. *Hmm...I guess there are lots of*

people out there who don't know about the King-dom... and there are probably more dragons, too! I think I should go to the...

Just then Seeker's mother, Contentment, called, "Seeker, will you come and help me, please?"

"Sure, Mom!" he answered. "Where are you?"

"The stairs to the attic!" she called. "Hurry!"

The attic was a little room at the very top of their house where Seeker's mother kept boxes of things which the family didn't need or use very often. When Seeker reached her, Contentment was halfway up and halfway down the stairs to the attic—with a bed! Seeker pushed on the bed and helped her to get it up the stairway.

Seeker looked around the attic room in surprise. Instead of boxes, there was a chest of drawers, a night table, and a lamp in the room. "Mom, what are you doing up here?"

"I'm changing this into a bedroom," she replied.

"Why?" asked Seeker.

"I don't know!" his mother answered.

"You don't know?!" he echoed.

4

Contentment shrugged her shoulders as she made the bed up with a fluffy warm comforter. "The King just told me to get it ready, so I am."

"This is great, Mom!" Seeker said, looking around at the cozy little room. "I wonder what the King has in mind. Didn't he even give you a hint?"

"No. He just told me to get it ready; and I've learned how much fun it is to trust him when he tells me to do something—especially when I don't understand why." Contentment smiled at Seeker and winked. "It's an adventure!"

"An adventure," Seeker nodded. "Mom, I just was on my way to the Secret Place when you called me. I'd better go now. See you later!"

CHAPTER TWO

When Seeker reached the Big Rock at the base of the Straight and Narrow Path, he was surprised to see his friends there: HopeSo, KnowSo, and Yes; Giggles, Gladness, and Glee; Doodle and Do...and they were all crowded around Dawdle and Slow.

"D-D-Don't w-w-worry about us," Dawdle was saying. "W-W-We'll be okay."

Seeker hurried over to his friends. "Dawdle and Slow! What happened?"

"Bullies," KnowSo explained. "Some kids have been picking on Dawdle and Slow again."

Seeker sighed and shook his head. Dawdle and Slow were different than most children. They talked and walked very, very slowly. Seeker and his friends had come to admire Dawdle and Slow because they were wise and cautious and took time to care about other people. But children who didn't know them often made fun of Dawdle and Slow and said very cruel words to them.

I'm on my way up to my Secret Place," Seeker said. "Why don't you all come with me and we'll talk to the King. He will help Dawdle and Slow!"

"I hope so!" said HopeSo.

"I KNOW so" agreed KnowSo.

"Yes, YES, of course he will!" Yes said with confidence.

The children greeted the Doorkeeper and then slid down the shining hallway. They all followed Seeker up the winding stairs to a room in one of the Castle's high towers. Seeker unlocked the door of his Secret Place. "Come on in everybody," he said.

Hardly a moment later, the door to the Secret Place opened quietly and the children looked up with delighted surprise. "King! You're here!" Giggles laughed hapily.

"He's always here," KnowSo explained knowingly, "We just don't always see him."

The King smiled and said, "Hi" in his deep kingly voice. "Hi, King," the children responded

"I came to talk to you about Moira, King," Seeker began. "She's really sad because of people living in the World Beyond the Kingdom."

The King nodded. "I know," he said.

"And I got feeling sad myself," Seeker continued. "I got to wondering how many people are out there who don't know you...they must feel sad, too."

"Speaking of sad," KnowSo interrupted, "We know some people right here who are sad!"

The children made way so that Dawdle and Slow could be next to the King. "M-M-My heart hurts, King," Dawdle said.

"M-M-Mine t-t-too," Slow nodded her agreement.

"I know," the King responded as he pulled Dawdle and Slow close to himself. "Here, let me touch your hearts." The King very gently touched Dawdle and Slow's hearts and they smiled.

"Th-th-thanks, King," Dawdle smiled.

Slow looked surprised. "W-W-Wow! I st-st-still remember the w-w-words that those kids said, b-b-but it d-d-doesn't hurt nearly as much anymore!"

Seeker had closely watched the King with Dawdle and Slow. *If only all those people out in the World Beyond the Kingdom could get to know the King,* he thought.

The King looked directly at Seeker, leaned forward, and winked. Then he reached out his hands to the children. "Come. I want to show you something."

The King led the children over to the Window of the Secret Place (a very special window where the King shows you things—the way they really are).

When Seeker and his friends looked out, they saw people. People were everywhere—little people, big people, old people, young people, and they were all busy. Some people were at school, some were working, some were at home, some were playing...

Then suddenly the picture changed, and the children saw the same people...but now they looked very different. Every single person was blind! And they were all bruised, and crippled, and hurting. Seeker and his friends could hear their cries...and, as they watched, they saw the reason for the people's pain.

Dragons! Hundreds of dragons. Thousands of dragons. All different colors, shapes, and sizes and every one of them was picking its nose! The children watched with disgust. "That is so gross!" Do exclaimed. "Why do they DO that, anyway?"

"Oh, I don't believe it!" Glee gasped. "That dragon over there—he blew his nose and didn't even use a tissue!"

"I think I'm going to be sick," Yes said, standing closer to the King.

A nasty odor reached the children's nostrils and they waved the air, frantically trying to get away from the smell. "Ugh!" cried Glee, holding her nose. "Don't they ever take a bath?!"

The dragons were breathing out puffs of incredibly bad breath, sneering, and muttering mean and nasty words. Some dragons wrapped chains around the people and wounded them. Other dragons put their slimy claws over the people's eyes and blinded them with a sort of oozing mucously screen; so they people could still see, but not *really* see...

The King spoke solemnly. "The dragons cripple the people and hurt them," he said. "The dragons keep the people blind so they can't see my Kingdom."

"That's awful!" Exclaimed HopeSo.

"That's terrible!" agreed KnowSo.

"Th-th-that's...sad," Dawdle and Slow said together.

But as Seeker looked through the Window, he realized that the sadness he had felt earlier had left him. Instead, he now felt *really* upset! Who did those dragons think they were, anyway?! Seeker turned to the King and spoke with fierce intensity. "So, what are we going to do about it, King?"

The King smiled at Seeker's courage and put a hand on his shoulder affectionately. "Well, Seeker, do you think you could bring *one* person out of the Darkness, away from the dragons, and into my Kingdom?"

Seeker looked out at the people and again heard their cries, and he looked at the dragons. Now they seemed even more terrible and disgusting. Seeker gulped, and slowly echoed the King's words. "One person...out of the Darkness...away from the dragons...into your kingdom..."

The other children looked at Seeker, then at the King, then back through the Window. For long moments they could hardly breathe. This certainly was a different kind of adventure! Seeker hesitated another moment then answered, "Okay, King—if you show me which one per-son, and if you REALLY help me!"

"I will help you," said King, "Look again."

13

CHAPTER THREE

Seeker and his friends looked through the Window of the Secret Place again, and saw that the scene had changed. There, on a hill not far from the Kingdom, was a young boy. He was about ten years old. He was walking along, kicking at rocks on the ground like a tough bully. Frowning a deep frown, his face looked dark and cloudy. Beside him were two ugly, hairy dragons. The King pointed and said, "Anger and Abuse. Those dragons have power over the boy. He is called 'NoName.' "

"H-H-How did that b-b-boy ever get like that, King?" asked Slow.

"Words," the King replied.

"W-W-Words?" Slow echoed questioningly as she glanced at her brother, Dawdle.

The King nodded, "Words can hurt very deeply. And unless you come to me with the pain, the dragons Anger and Abuse will begin to take control. Look at NoName again. You will see some of the reasons why he acts the way he does."

Through the Window of the Secret Place the children were able to see some of NoName's life. They saw him at school and listened as a group of mean children spoke cruel words to him. They saw his embarrassment as a teacher made fun of his failing grade on a test in front of the entire class. And Seeker and his friends watched in dismay as NoName went to his home where his mother said even more cruel words to him and treated him in mean and hurtful ways.

The dragons Anger and Abuse were always close to NoName, and each time cruel words were spoken, the nasty dragons tightened chains around the boy and smeared his eyes with blinding mucous.

As Seeker and his friends continued to watch, they realized that they could hear the cry that was within the boy's heart. On the outside he was a mean bully, but inside, he was full of pain. On the outside he was mumbling curses, but inside he was singing a very sad song...

"My name is NoName;
I am blind and I can't see;
But sometime, somewhere
I just know that I will be—
Someone, 'cause somehow
Somebody
Is gonna come and be...my friend."

Then the dragons and their chains vanished, and there was the young boy again, kicking the ground, and acting tough. But now the children understood that he wasn't really tough at all; he was just hurt and lonely.

"King!" Seeker cried with excitement, "I'll be his friend! I'll be his friend!"

"All right, Seeker," responded the King, "But remember—he doesn't believe in me, so he is unable to see my Kingdom. The dragons have blinded his eyes...but I give you power over the dragons." The King reached out and gently put his hands on Seeker's head and said, "Seeker, I give you power to bring NoName to me!"

"Yes Sir!" Seeker saluted.

"What can we DO, King?" Doodle asked excitedly.

"You can wear your armor!" The King smiled one of his mysterious smiles and picked up a copy of the Great Book from where the children had been sitting. (The King had previously given Seeker and his friends their own copy of the Great Book and they always brought it along to read in the Secret Place.) The King opened the Book to the page he wanted and smiled again, "Ah, yes. Here it is: The Armor of Light!" As soon as the King spoke, the children saw a cabinet in the corner of the Secret Place that they had never noticed before. The King opened the door of the cabinet and pulled out pieces of shining armor. Seeker and his friends' eyes grew wide. "Wow," they breathed.

"This," declared the King, "is the Armor of Light. You must wear it at all times. It will keep you safe from the dragons and it will make you strong soldiers in my army!"

"We're in the army again, King?!" they asked. (They were remembering an earlier time when the children of the Kingdom had marched forth as soldiers and defeated the dragon Greed by giving and sharing.)

The King laughed. "You've never left my army! You are just learning more about what it really means to be soldiers! Now, let's get you dressed for battle!

"This is a breastplate—to protect your heart and to help you do what is right. With it, wear this belt called Truth. And here are army shoes. Put them on and always be ready to run and tell people the good news of my Kingdom! Wear this helmet to protect your minds. Remember that you belong to me and nothing can harm you!"

As the King helped them put on the Armor of Light, two things amazed Seeker and his friends. First of all, they realized that the armor fit them perfectly; and secondly, once the armor was on, they couldn't see it anymore!

The King noticed their expressions and laughed. "You wear my armor by believing in it. Every day I want you to take each piece and put it on, knowing that although you can't see it; it is really there! And, also know this—even though you can't see it, the dragons can!"

18

Seeker stood tall, his eyes shining. "Maybe I can't see the Armor of Light, King, but I can feel it!"

The King smiled and said, "This is your shield. It is called Faith. Use it to fight off the lies of the dragons. Believe that I am the King and I am with you!"

Then the King handed a sparkling sword to each child, which like the other pieces of armor, disappeared from sight as they took hold of it. "Your Sword is the Great Book," explained the King. "As you speak my words, those words will pierce the enemy."

The King put his hands on Dawdle and Slow's hearts, where the shining breastplates fit closely around their chests. "Words have great power. They can hurt...or they can heal. They can bring chains of anger and abuse, or they can set people free. Wear your armor every day. It will help you keep cruel words from penetrating your hearts. As you speak MY words and refuse to listen to words that hurt, you will be strong soldiers in my army..."

Dawdle and Slow's eyes sparkled as even more of the pain in their hearts was washed away. "Th-Thanks, King!"

"You are all strong soldiers!" the King declared in his most kingly voice. "Seeker will go out and rescue NoName from the dragons. The rest of you must stand guard here in the Secret Place. Stay alert, and watch over him carefully. The Secret Place is where many great battles are fought...and won...for my Kingdom. Study the words of the Great Book. Watch through the Window

everyday and I will show you the way things really are—
not the way they appear to be."

"Yes sir!" the children said as they saluted.

The King again put his hands on Seeker and smiled,
"According to the words of my Great Book: 'The Spirit of
the King is upon you! I have given you power to tell the
good news; to heal the brokenhearted; to set prisoners free
and make blind eyes see!' Now, GO!"

Seeker bowed before the King, then stood at attention
and saluted. "Yes sir!"

CHAPTER FOUR

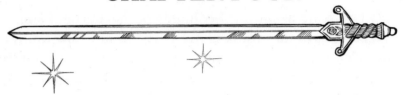

Seeker ran out from the Secret Place, down the tower steps, and through the castle gardens. He was so filled with a sense of adventure that he was completely surprised when his sister called to him, "Hey! Where are you going in such a hurry?"

"Moira!" Seeker cried, screeching to a halt. "What are you doing here?"

"Spending time in my Secret Place," Moira explained. "It's right over there–the bench under that tree. I've just been talking to the King about my friend, Loneliness. So, where are you going?"

"I'm going on an adventure! I'm going to meet NoName! And look at my Armor of Light!" Seeker pointed proudly to his breastplate.

Moira was puzzled. "NoName? Who's that? And what is the Armor of Light? I don't see any armor!"

"Maybe you can't see it, but it's there! Listen, Moira, I'm in a real hurry! You can find out about the Armor of Light in the King's Great Book. See you later!" And with that, Seeker raced toward the hill that was not too far from the Kingdom.

The path up the hill was overgrown and hard to climb. Seeker had to pause several times to catch his breath. It took him longer than he expected, and when he finally neared the top, he was relieved to see that NoName was still there—kicking at rocks and looking "tough."

Seeker ran toward him, panting. "Hi!" He called excitedly.

But to Seeker's amazement, NoName was not happy to see him. He turned toward Seeker with a stormy glare and shouted, "Stay away from me, kid! Take off!"

Seeker stopped running. He waited a few more minutes to catch his breath, then approached the boy more cautiously. "Uh...hello there...uh...my name is Seeker. What's yours?"

"I said 'take off'!"

"Take Off? Hmm...that's a nice name; maybe I'll call you T.O. for short!" Seeker laughed at his clever joke; but then noticed that he was the only one laughing.

NoName turned on him and spoke angrily. "Get that stupid grin off your face! Boy are you ugly! Get away from here, you shrimpy kid!"

For a moment, Seeker didn't know what to do. *I'm sure glad I have the Armor of Light he thought to himself. Words like that used to hurt me, but not anymore! King, please help me...*Then Seeker got an idea. He cleared his throat and said in a friendly voice, "So...Do you like rocks?!"

"Do I like rocks!?" NoName echoed in disgust. "What do you mean—'Do I like rocks?!' What kind of dumb question is that?"

"Well, I just noticed you up here on the hill kicking the rocks. I know how to skip rocks—you know, make them dance across the water. The King taught me."

"Don't give me that stuff about a King!" NoName sneered. "There's no such thing as a King!"

"Oh, yes there is!" Seeker replied, "And he did teach me how to skip rocks...and I'm going to teach you too!"

To NoName's great surprise, Seeker grabbed his hand and raced down the hill. (It's hard to stop when you are running down a hill!) At the bottom of the hill, near the bridge to the Kingdom, was a stream where Seeker had spent many hours with the King.

Seeker searched the shore and quickly found some nice, round, smooth stones and showed them to NoName.

24

"See? You have to use these kind—they remind me of little pancakes!"

"Pancake rocks," NoName sneered, "Who cares?"

Seeker went over to the stream and bent down. He made sure his arm was at the right angle, then tossed the first stone. It danced happily across the top of the water for a short distance, then sank.

Seeker turned to NoName and handed him a stone. "Here! Give it a try!"

NoName shrugged and took the stone, "You're not going to leave me alone until I do, right? Oh, all right, why not dance a pancake rock?" He bent down and threw the stone. It immediately sank. NoName turned away in anger, "See?! I knew I couldn't do it! Who cares anyway?!"

Seeker reached out and took NoName's arm to stop him from leaving. "Don't give up so fast!" Seeker said, "Let me show you!"

Seeker picked up another stone. "Look," he said, "Keep your arm parallel to the water, and when you toss the stone, flick your wrist...like this..." NoName rolled his eyes and sighed a deep sigh as if trying to tell Seeker how boring this was. Then he took the stone Seeker offered, sighed another bored sigh, and sent the stone skimming over the water. Skip...skip...skip... "You did it!" Seeker cried, "It skipped three times! That was great!"

26

NoName shrugged and tried to act uninterested as he reached down to pick up another stone. "So...uh...is this one flat enough?" NoName caught on quickly after that, and because he was so strong, one of his stones went skimming across the surface of the water all the way to the other shore!

Seeker was very impressed. "Wow! That rock got all the way over to the Kingdom!" He paused thoughtfully, then said, "It's a great place, you know, the Kingdom...That's where the King..."

NoName interrupted quickly. "Yeah right," he said. "Listen kid—no fake stories, okay? Don't give me any of that Kingdom stuff—it's all a bunch of lies." NoName bent to pick up two stones, and handed one to Seeker. "Are you up to a challenge?"

Seeker laughed as he and NoName sent the rocks flying across the water. They skipped rocks for a while longer, and then NoName turned to leave. "I have to go now," he said. He walked a short distance, then turned back toward Seeker and looked at him for a long moment. He seemed uncomfortable. Seeker just waited patiently until NoName finally spoke. "Uh...would you...I mean...do you uh...want to skip rocks again tomorrow?"

Seeker smiled. "Sure! I'll meet you on the hill!" NoName nodded and walked away.

Seeker waited until NoName was out of sight, then put both thumbs up happily, "Thanks, King! And thanks to all my friends for watching out for me from the Secret Place!"

And that was the beginning of a great friendship. Every day Seeker would go to the Secret Place to talk to the King and put on his armor; and every day he would meet NoName on the hill. The two boys built tree houses and forts and explored the forests near the Kingdom. Sometimes they skipped rocks at the steam or went fishing.

Weeks and months passed. Gradually, the dark and cloudy expression on NoName's face was replaced by a soft sort of friendliness.

"No sign of the dragons anywhere!" Seeker happily reported to his friends one day in the Secret Place. "I think Anger and Abuse have really lost their grip on NoName!"

But Seeker's friends shook their heads. "No, Seeker," warned KnowSo. "Those dragons are still close by. Make sure you wear your armor."

Doodle nodded, "And tell NoName about the King, Seeker! Don't give up. The truth about the King will set him free from the dragons."

Do pointed to the Great Book. "Look, that's what it says right here! The truth will set him free. DO it, Seeker! Tell NoName the truth. Don't give up!"

That was good advice, because lately, Seeker *had* given up trying to talk to NoName about the King. Every time Seeker had brought up the subject, NoName refused to listen. "I don't believe in all that stuff," he would say, and then mutter angrily under his breath about "fake Kingdom stories."

The next day, after Doodle and Do's encouragement, Seeker had an idea. He and NoName were carrying their fishing poles over their shoulders and walking barefoot across a log to their favorite fishing spot. As they walked, Seeker thought to himself, *He won't let me talk about the King, but he never told me not to sing about the King! It's worth a try...*

When the boys had settled on the bank of the stream and sank their hooks in the water, Seeker leaned back against a tree and casually began to sing one of the King's songs...

"There is a King who loves you....
There is a King who cares..."

NoName reacted immediately, "Quit it, Seeker! I don't like that kind of music!" Seeker pretended to be hurt, and NoName added quickly, "Besides, you're scaring the fish away!"

"Okay, okay!" Seeker said defensively, "I'll just hum it! Maybe the fish will like that!"

Seeker quietly hummed the tune over and over. He glanced over at NoName from time to time with a smile. NoName shook his head at his friend, but Seeker was sure that he saw NoName smiling, too.

CHAPTER FIVE

Time passed in the Kingdom of Joy and Peace. As the children continued to meet together in the Secret Place, Seeker's sister Moira, also spent time in her Secret Place in the King's Gardens. The King had given her a copy of the Great Book, and the words seemed like they were alive. Every day Moira read and read and read. She, too, had discovered the Armor of Light and had learned to put it on each day. Moira was happier than she had ever been, but her happiness was always shadowed by the sorrow she felt for Loneliness.

One day, in her Secret Place, Moira was talking to the King about her friend. "Well. King, here I am again. It's been a long time, but I'll just keep asking you about Loneliness. Please, please, please help her to find the way into your Kingdom. She needs you so much. Please help her...and help her little boy. Rescue them from the

Darkness...Help them know the truth about you and to get rid of the lies the dragons have told them..."

Just then, Moira heard someone crying. To her surprise, Slow was walking toward her on the path. "Why, Slow," she said as she went over to the young girl, "What's wrong?"

But Slow couldn't answer. She just cried harder. Moira gave her a tissue and helped her sit down on the bench. After quite a long time, Slow finally said, "W-W-Words."

"Words?" Moira echoed.

Slow nodded. "W-W-Words really hurt. I-I wish that Dawdle and I could talk b-b-better and w-w-walk better. Then people wouldn't s-s-say such mean things to us."

Moira shook her head, "No, Slow. Cruel words can be spoken to you even if you talk and walk the same as other people. It's what you DO when the words are spoken— that's what matters. Have you been wearing your armor?"

Slow nodded, then shook her head, "S-S-Sometimes I forget. And sometimes...well, sometimes, I just feel t-t-too young to be a s-s-soldier.

"Sometimes...like today?" Moira asked gently.

Slow nodded and smiled as she blew her nose again. "But I know that's not right. Little soldiers can be very powerful in the King's army." Then after a long sigh, Slow continued. "I feel better. Thanks, Moira. I think I'm ready to go back to the Secret Place and get my armor! I didn't put it on yet today."

"You can put it on right here!" Moira smiled. "The Secret Place is wherever you meet with the King. All you have to do is call his name, and he will be with you—although you might not see him!" Moira opened the Great Book and pointed, "Here is where it explains about the Armor of Light. You take each piece and put it on; even though you can't see it, it is really there! Look...a helmet, a sword...even boots for those soldiers who happen to have little feet!"

Slow laughed and was marching around the King's Gardens when Dawdle suddenly burst through one of the shrubs. He spoke more quickly than he had ever spoken before, "Hu-Hurry, Slow!" he panted, "Emer-mergency meeting in the Secret Place! S-S-Seeker is in trouble!"

CHAPTER SIX

Earlier that day Seeker had made the same mistake Slow had made: he hadn't put on his armor.

Things are going so great with NoName, he had thought to himself. *Those dragons are miles away from here now! And pretty soon, NoName is going to just start believing the truth, and everything's going to be just fine!* So, instead of taking time in the Secret Place, Seeker just whistled happily on his way across the Kingdom bridge to meet NoName.

When Seeker arrived at the hill, NoName was sitting in the grass, waiting for him. "Seeker, sit down for a minute," NoName said, patting the ground beside him. "I've been thinking about you, Seeker. I've been thinking about you a lot. And I've been wondering...well... uh...what are you seeking for?"

"What am I seeking for?" Seeker echoed thoughtfully as he sat down, "Hmm, I guess just to know more about the King…Yeah, I'm seeking to know more about the King."

"But, Seeker, you don't REALLY believe in that stuff about a King, do you?" asked NoName.

"Oh yes!!" replied Seeker, "I REALLY believe in it! It's the truth!"

NoName looked at his friend, then continued, "The truth, huh? So, tell me IF there IS a King, where does he live?"

"Why, right over there in the Castle!" Seeker stood and pointed. His heart began to beat faster as he realized what was happening. *This is so great! I just knew he was close to believing the truth!*

NoName stood up and peered intently in the direction Seeker pointed. "What Castle? I just see trees!"

"Oh yeah, you can't see it yet," said Seeker, remembering that NoName's eyes had been blinded by the dragons. "Well, there really is a Castle, NoName, and there really is a King! And he REALLY loves you!"

NoName peered harder and said earnestly, "He does?!"

Suddenly, it was as though Seeker was looking through the Window of the Secret Place. He saw NoName the same way he had seen him that first day—crippled, bruised, and wounded; with chains wrapped all around him. But now, the chains were much looser than they had been, and his eyes weren't covered with the oozing mucously screen—they were starting to open!

Seeker was so happy that he laughed and hugged NoName. "Your eyes are starting to open! This is so great! You're starting to understand!"

"I am?" NoName asked, "Yeah…I guess I am!"

NoName rubbed his eyes and looked again toward the Kingdom, "I think I can see a Castle! Yes, I DO see the Castle! Wow! It's so white it sparkles! This is awesome!"

"Yes!" Seeker cried happily. "Very, very awesome!"

But suddenly, the air became cool, the sky darkened, and as if appearing from nowhere, Anger and Abuse came raging up the hill toward the two boys. And it was then that Seeker realized he didn't have on the Armor of Light.

The fiery green breath of Anger and Abuse smelled as though they had never, ever brushed their teeth and their breath burned Seeker's heart as they snarled past him toward NoName. The dragons put their claws over the boy's eyes, blinding him once again with their oozing mucous. They tightened the chains with a determined pull, and then, with terrifying fierceness, the dragons roared at Seeker.

NoName stood on the hill, angry and confused. He looked at Seeker; then stepped back, shook his head, and cried, "Lies! Lies! Listen Seeker, don't you ever talk to me about the King again! I don't believe it! It's not the truth! I don't believe it! Get away from me! Never come near me again with your stupid Kingdom stories! Get away from me!"

With that, NoName lifted his hand to hit Seeker. Seeker dodged just in time. Fear rose up within Seeker's heart. NoName's face was dark with an evil sort of cloudiness. *The dragons,* Seeker thought in horror, *The dragons have control of him! And here I am without my armor!* Seeker dodged another swoop of NoName's fists.

"NoName!" he cried, "It's me, Seeker! Please, just listen to me!" Seeker dodged yet another blow. "NoName, please! I'm your friend, remember?"

It was at that moment that Moira, Dawdle, and Slow reached the Secret Place. "Hurry!" HopeSo cried, "Seeker is trying to fight the battle alone."

The children gathered at the window and peered through the Darkness to see Seeker dodging NoName's fists.

"He forgot to wear his armor," Do said.

"And he forgot to take his sword," Doodle added, holding up Seeker's copy of the Great Book that was lying in the Secret Place. "He's trying to use his own words, but his own words aren't powerful enough."

Moira nodded. "He needs to use the KING'S words."

"Yes!" Yes cried. "He needs to use his sword!"

"C-C-Can we take it to him?" Dawdle wondered. "Or d-d-does he need to come h-h-here to the Secret Place to get it?"

Slow shot a smile toward Moira, "He c-can have a Secret Place right where he is. He just n-needs to call out to the King!"

Moira smiled back and then said, "Listen everyone, the Great Book says there is power when two or more ask something in the Secret Place together. Let's ask, together, for Seeker to call on the King."

"Okay, Moira," the children nodded.

"We'll DO it!" announced Doodle.

The children joined hands with Moira, and with one voice, they shouted through the Window of the Secret Place, "Call upon the King! Seeker, call upon the King!"

By now, NoName had dropped down on the ground. He was pounding his fists into the grass, and crying, but refused to let Seeker come near. Anger and Abuse were picking their noses, sneering wickedly, and pulling the chains tighter around the young boy. *I don't know what to do,* Seeker thought. *I can't just leave him here! And it's gotten so dark! I don't know if I could even find my way back to the Kingdom bridge! I need help...I need...the King! Of course! What have I been thinking?* Seeker closed his eyes tightly and whispered, "King! King, please help me! I'm so sorry for not putting on my armor..."

"Then put it on now!" said a familiar voice.

Seeker wheeled around in surprise. There, in the middle of the Darkness, stood the King. "King! You're here!" Seeker cried as he hugged the King in relief. "But how can I put on my armor? I left it in the Secret Place!"

The King smiled. "The Secret Place is wherever you meet with me, Seeker. Now go ahead, put your armor on! The King handed each piece of armor to Seeker, and then leaned forward, winked, and disappeared from his sight. As Seeker put on his armor, he immediately felt stronger. He stood tall, and his eyes were shining as he turned back toward NoName...and Anger and Abuse.

The dragons had been watching.

They had watched the King appear...then disappear. They had watched Seeker put on the Armor of Light. And, as the dragons watched, they had become very, very afraid. "Uh-oh," they said anxiously, their bad breath coming in nervous gasps. They still had firm grips on the chains around NoName, but their claws were shaking so badly that they couldn't even pick their noses.

When Seeker turned toward them, Anger and Abuse tried their best to look fierce and unafraid. They roared loudly and tightened the chains around NoName, who cried out with pain so deep that suddenly, Seeker became absolutely furious. "Leave him alone! Do you hear me, dragons?" he shouted. "NoName was just starting to see— just starting to understand! His eyes were just beginning to open!" Seeker stomped his foot and cried, "I've had it with you dragons!"

The dragons belched rudely. "And we've had it with you, too!" they mocked. "The kid stays with us!" Anger and Abuse pulled the chains more tightly around NoName.

Then Seeker heard the King's voice speaking to him. "Don't hold a conversation with them, Seeker," the King said. "I have given you power to bring NoName into my Kingdom. You have power over those dragons! Go ahead, Seeker!"

Seeker felt strength from the King's words. "Oh yeah! Power! The King has given me power!" Seeker rolled up his shirtsleeves, adjusted the Armor of Light (which he couldn't see but knew was there), clenched his fists, and called out with confident authority, "DRAGONS!"

The dragons looked around anxiously, desperately trying to pick their noses while hanging on to NoName.

"DRAGONS!" Seeker repeated, "I order you to get your claws off that kid right now!"

Seeker's words came with such force that the dragons yelled out in pain; but they continued their hold on NoName.

Seeker's heart filled with determination. He rolled his sleeves up a bit farther, took a deep breath, and said in a low, meaningful voice, "Now you listen here, dragons!

The King has given me POWER over you! I said get your claws off that kid right now!" The dragons cried out again with pain, but still held tightly to NoName.

The King spoke quietly. "Use your sword, Seeker."

Without seeing it, but knowing it was there, Seeker held out his sword. With great authority in his voice, he declared words from the Great Book. "The Spirit of the King is upon me! He has given me power to tell his good news; to heal the brokenhearted; to set prisoners free and make blind eyes see! In the Name of the King, dragons—GO!"

Although he didn't realize it, Seeker's friends and his sister, Moira, were speaking the same words from the Great Book. And as they spoke, they saw a Light more brilliant then any light. The Light cut right through the Darkness and wrapped itself protectively around NoName. "The people who walked in Darkness have seen a great Light!" Moira cried. "Those who walked in the dragon's land—upon them the Light has shined!"

Meanwhile, the dragons frantically held their ears and cried out in pain. The words from the Great Book pierced and cut their grip on the chains surrounding NoName. The Light pushed them backwards, and with each powerful word from the Great book, Anger and Abuse grew smaller, and smaller, and smaller. They moaned in agony until, with one final whimper of defeat, the dragons slithered away.

Seeker watched, and then realized how very tired he felt. With a deep sigh, he leaned on his sword and sank down onto his knees. After a few moments, Seeker looked across the hill toward NoName. What he saw brought a flood of tears to his eyes.

Light covered the hillside. NoName was rubbing his eyes and laughing and crying all at the same time. His eyes were finally open and he was looking at the one who had broken the dragons' power, the one who lived in the Light...the one who really, really loved him....

And in the next instant, NoName ran into the arms of the King.

CHAPTER SEVEN

"NoName and the King!" Seeker whispered. "NoName and the King! Hey, why am I whispering? I should be yelling with everything I've got to yell with!" Seeker began jumping up and down and shouting, "NoName and the King! Hey, dragons! Hey, everybody in the Secret Place—look! Hey, everybody in the whole world! NoName and the King! They're finally together! Hooray! Hooray! NoName and the King!"

Seeker started doing cartwheels across the hillside. In the Secret Place, all of his friends were jumping up and down and yelling, too. Then Moira said, "Shhh!" and called them all to look again through the Window of the Secret Place. Seeker turned at the same time, and realized that the King was singing.

The King was singing the most beautiful song that NoName had ever heard. The words of the song were words from the Great book—powerful words that brought healing and strength to every place where, throughout NoName's life, other words had torn and bruised and crippled him.

As the King sang, he removed the chains. He healed what had been bruised and broken. And NoName was brought out of Darkness into the Kingdom of Light.

I was once wounded...like you.
I was once wounded for you;
I felt your pain;
I took your pain.

I am acquainted with sorrow.
I was despised and rejected;
I was hurt, and afflicted;
I took your grief,
So that you might have peace;
I bore your sins and transgressions.

Now you are healed—I am your healer.
You are healed—I make you whole.
See the chains fall aside;
I have opened your eyes;
And behold, I am your healer.

The King helped the boy to his feet, and put an arm around his shoulders. Then the King looked over at Seeker and waved for him to come. Seeker hurried across the hill. While the King smiled one of his mysterious smiles, the two friends hugged, laughed and cried together.

"This is so great!" Seeker said. "This is just so great!"

"Seeker," said the King, "This—is 'NewName'!"

"NewName?!" echoed Seeker. "Wow! Welcome to the Kingdom! This is just so great!"

The boys hugged again. "Thanks for being my friend, Seeker," NewName said. "Thanks for telling me about the King. And thanks for not giving up."

Seeker gave his friend a handclap, then looked closely at his eyes. "Can you see the Castle now? No more trees?! Can you see the Castle?"

"I can see it, Seeker. I really can!"

"Okay. Look harder. There's one especially tall tower —it's my Secret Place!"

"Secret Place?" NewName squinted and strained to see, "I think I see an especially tall tower...but all the towers look pretty special to me!"

"Well anyway, my friends and I have been meeting there and doing battles against the dragons this whole time! And we've learned all about the Armor of Light and..."

"Dragons?" NewName echoed. "What dragons? Armor of Light? What's that?"

"You'll find out, NewName!" Seeker said happily. "Wow, King, what an adventure this has been!"

"And it's not over yet, Seeker," the King said as he put his great arms around both boys and smiled a most mysterious smile. "NewName needs a place to live for awhile. Do you happen to know where he could stay?"

51

"What?" Seeker asked, confused. "No, I don't think so...but I'm sure we could find someplace."

The King smiled again, "Hmmm...Well, I thought you might just know of a nice, cozy little room that's just waiting for someone like NewName to move into."

"Nice, cozy little room?" Seeker echoed. His mind went blank for a moment; then Seeker looked up at the King with wide-open eyes. The attic room! Of course! "Yeah, King! Yeah, I sure do know a nice, cozy little room! My mom changed the attic room into a bedroom...just like you told her to, King! You had it planned out all along, didn't you?! Wow. This is all so great. NewName can stay at our place!" He turned to NewName excitedly, "You can stay with us!"

The King nodded. "That's good, Seeker. Because your sister, Moira, has been spending time with me in her Secret Place...talking to me about NewName's mother...."

At this, Moira leaned farther through the Window to hear the King speak. "NewName's mother?" she echoed out loud. "But I don't know NewName's mother! What does the King mean?"

The King looked through the Window of the Secret Place at Moira, winked, and continued speaking. "Moira has been talking to me about NewName's mother. Her name is Loneliness. And I am going to meet her...right now."

Land of Laws Forgotten

Island of Despair

ROYAL HARBOR

GENEROSITY

Valley of Lost Dreams

Talking Tree Forest

World Beyond the Kingdom

The Kingdom of Joy and Peace

N E S W

THINK ABOUT THE STORY

Do you know anyone like NoName? Do you know someone who looks and acts tough on the outside? It is probably because they are hurting on the inside. It is probably because they need a friend. Go to the Secret Place! Let the King show you how to pray; let Him give you the power and the spiritual tools you need to bring people out of the Darkness, to Him.

Or, perhaps you yourself are like NoName. Perhaps you have been full of anger and abuse, pain and hurt on the inside. King Jesus can heal you.

SEARCH THE PAGES OF THE KING'S GREAT BOOK...

Matthew 6:6—Go into the Secret Place
Jeremiah 33:3—Let the King show you things.
Romans 13:12—The "Armor of Light"
Ephesians 6:11-17—The pieces of armor
Isaiah 53:3-5—The King suffered...for you
Luke 4:18—Healing for broken hearts; sight
for the blind

TALK TO THE KING

"King Jesus, You see the real me. People see the outside; but You see my heart. You know the anger, the bitterness, the pain, and the loneliness that I feel sometimes. Well, today, I ask You to help me. I give you all my feelings. Please help me to forgive people who have said or done things to me that were mean or wrong. Help me to be clothed in Your Armor of Light every day. And please help me to bring Your healing to the hurting people around me. I want my life to truly be an ADVENTURE! Help me to be a SEEKER!"

A VERSE TO REMEMBER...

The King came to heal the broken hearted
and to set the prisoners free!
He opens up the eyes that were blinded.
Look at Luke chapter 4:18.

Adventures in the Kingdom™
by Dian Layton

━━ SEEKER'S GREAT ADVENTURE
Seeker and his friends leave the CARNALville of Selfishness and begin the great adventure of really knowing the King!

━━ RESCUED FROM THE DRAGON
The King needs an army to conquer a very disgusting dragon and rescue the people who live in the Village of Greed.

━━ SECRET OF THE BLUE POUCH
The children of the Kingdom explore the pages of an ancient golden book and step through a most remarkable doorway — into a brand new kind of adventure!

━━ IN SEARCH OF WANDERER
Come aboard the sailing ship *The Adventurer*, and find out how Seeker learns to fight dragons through the window of the Secret Place.

━━ THE DREAMER
Moira, Seeker's older sister, leaves the Kingdom and disappears into the Valley of Lost Dreams. Can Seeker rescue his sister before it's too late?

━━ ARMOR OF LIGHT
In the World Beyond the Kingdom, Seeker must use the King's weapons to fight the dragons Bitterness and Anger to save the life of one young boy.

━━ CARRIERS OF THE KINGDOM
Seeker and his friends discover that the Kingdom is within them! In the Land of Laws Forgotten they meet with Opposition, and the children battle against some very nasty dragons who do not want the people to remember...

Available at your local Christian bookstore.

**For more information and sample chapters,
visit www.destinyimage.com or www.seeker.org**

Now Join Seeker

& His Friends

in an Exciting
Sunday School
Curriculum!

Learn New
Things
About the
King and Get
to Know Him
Better
at
Seeker.org

The Young God Chasers
Curriculum Series by Dian Layton

▬ Seeking the King

(With quotes and concepts from *The God Chasers* by Tommy Tenney) Many children who attend church "live in the Kingdom, but don't know the King." A God Chaser is a "SEEKER"! The lessons in this first binder are designed to encourage hunger in the children's hearts to really KNOW (not just know ABOUT) King Jesus!

▬ The King and His Kingdom

(With quotes and concepts from *The God Chasers* by Tommy Tenney) Children need to hear what is on the King's heart and then DO what He tells them to do...not just "some day when they grow up"; but NOW! Children can be part of His "very big little army" and have a powerful impact on the world around them!

▬ Seeker's Sources of Power

(With quotes and concepts from *Secret Sources of Power* by Tommy Tenney) The concept of having POWER is intriguing to children. How valuable for youngsters to learn that the true source of power is being emptied of self and filled up with Jesus! They will learn how to live a POWER-FILLED life every day!

▬ Seeker's Secret Place

(With quotes and concepts from *Secret Sources of Power* by Tommy Tenney) Many people spend time in counseling sessions trying to get free of the guilt, worry, fear, and sin they have been carrying around for years. In this curriculum, children learn how to "cast all their cares" and "unload their heavy burdens" on Jesus.

Watch for these titles at your local Christian bookstore.